ALPHABAKE

• • • • • • • • • • • • • • • • •

A COOKBOOK AND
COOKIE CUTTER SET

BY DEBORA PEARSON

ILLUSTRATED BY JANE KURISU

Dutton Children's Books
New York

Library of Congress Cataloging-in-Publication Data

Pearson, Debora.
    The alphabake cookbook and cookie cutter set / by Debora Pearson;
illustrated by Jane Kurisu. — 1st ed.
        p.   cm.
ISBN 0-525-45461-6
1. Cookies—Juvenile literature. [1. Cookies.] I. Kurisu, Jane, date ill. II. Title
    TX772.P35   1995
    641.8'654—dc20   95-13379   CIP   AC

Published in the United States 1995
by Dutton Children's Books,
a division of Penguin Books USA Inc.
375 Hudson Street, New York, New York 10014

Designed by Brenda van Ginkel

Produced by Somerville House Books Limited
3080 Yonge Street, Suite 5000
Toronto, Ontario, Canada
M4N 3N1

Printed in Hong Kong   First Edition

5 7 9 10 8 6 4

Answers to puzzles in the book:

Page 25: The D objects are a Dalmatian dog, dishes, dough, daffodils, a duck, a doll.

Page 27: <u>s</u>oup, <u>j</u>am, <u>p</u>eanut butter, <u>m</u>ilk

2

·TABLE OF CONTENTS·

A Safety Reminder

The recipes and activities in this book are for

adults and children to do together. Before you start to bake,

ask your mom, dad, or another grown-up to help you.

Ask your helper to make sure that pots on top of the stove have

their handles turned away from the edge so that no one

bumps into them. Your grown-up helper can also show you the

safe way to take things out of the oven, using oven mitts or

pot holders. Always be very careful when you are around a stove

or oven. Never handle anything hot with your bare hands.

It's time to make some cookies! Here's what you'll need:

MIXING BOWLS

MEASURING
SPOONS

MEASURING CUP

MIXING SPOON

PLASTIC WRAP
OR WAXED PAPER

ROLLING PIN

POT

SPATULA

OVEN MITTS
OR POT HOLDERS

ALPHABAKE COOKIE
CUTTERS

ALPHABAKE COOKIE
SHEET

·ALPHABAKE COOKIES·

Here is the basic recipe you follow to make all the
different cookies in this book. If you have any questions as you use
the other recipes, you can look at these pictures to see how
each step is done. You can also use this recipe just as it is here,
without adding anything else or doing anything more.

WHAT YOU NEED:

$^1/_2$ cup (125 mL or 1 stick) butter or
    margarine, softened
$^3/_4$ cup (175 mL) white sugar
1 egg
1 teaspoon (5 mL) vanilla extract

$1^1/_2$ cups (375 mL) all-purpose flour
$^1/_2$ teaspoon (2 mL) baking powder
$^1/_4$ teaspoon (1 mL) salt
cooking spray or extra butter for
    greasing the cookie sheet

WHAT YOU DO:

1 Mix the butter
and sugar
together in
a big bowl
until they
are creamy.

2 Add the egg
and vanilla
extract to
the bowl.
Mix again.

3 In another bowl, stir the flour,
baking powder, and salt together.

4 Bit by bit, add the flour mixture to the bowl with the butter mixture and mix until smooth.

5 Pat the dough into a ball and wrap it in plastic wrap or waxed paper. Put the dough in the freezer for about 15 minutes.

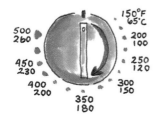

6 Preheat the oven to 350°F (180°C). Grease your cookie sheet with the cooking spray or extra butter.

150°F
65°C

500
260

450
230

400
200

350
180

300
150

250
120

200
100

7 Roll out the dough on a floured surface until it is half as thick as your Alphabake cookie cutters. Cut out the dough, using any of your Alphabake letters.

8 Gently remove the extra dough around the dough letters. Put the cookies on your cookie sheet, leaving a space as wide as three of your fingers between each one.

9 Bake the cookies for about 10 to 12 minutes. Let the cookies cool before eating.

·YOU-NAME-IT COOKIES·

Find the Alphabake letters that spell your name,
then use them to make special cookies just for you. You can also
make the names of people you know and surprise them!

WHAT YOU NEED:

1/2 cup (125 mL or 1 stick) butter or margarine, softened

3/4 cup (175 mL) white sugar

1 egg

1 teaspoon (5 mL) vanilla extract

1 1/2 cups (375 mL) all-purpose flour

1/2 teaspoon (2 mL) baking powder

1/4 teaspoon (1 mL) salt

cooking spray or extra butter for greasing the cookie sheet

WHAT YOU DO:

1 Mix the butter and sugar together in a big bowl until they are creamy.

2 Add the egg and vanilla extract to the bowl. Mix again.

3 In another bowl, stir the flour, baking powder, and salt together.

4 Bit by bit, add the flour mixture to the bowl with the butter mixture and mix until smooth.

5 Pat the dough into a ball and wrap it in plastic wrap or waxed paper. Put the dough in the freezer for about 15 minutes.

6 Preheat the oven to 350°F (180°C). Grease your cookie sheet with the cooking spray or extra butter.

7 Roll out the dough on a floured surface until it is half as thick as your Alphabake cookie cutters. Cut out the dough, using the cookie cutters that spell your name.

8 Gently remove the extra dough around the dough letters. Put the cookies on your cookie sheet, leaving a space as wide as three of your fingers between each one.

9 Bake the cookies for about 10 to 12 minutes. Let the cookies cool before eating.

·Handy Hint·

Dip your cookie cutters in flour first so they don't stick to the dough!

·MORE YOU-NAME-IT FUN·

You can make a big cookie with your name on it!

Roll out a piece of dough large enough to hold
the letters of your name or your initials, but not bigger than your cookie sheet.
Lift the dough and put it on the cookie sheet.

Cut out your name or initials, using the cookie
cutters. Pull the dough letters off, leaving the big piece
of dough on the sheet. Can you see your name?

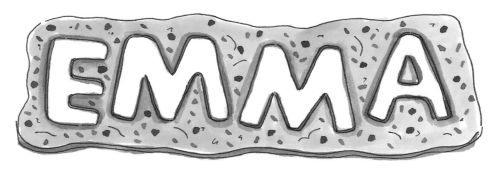

Decorate your big cookie with chocolate chips, sprinkles, sunflower seeds,
colored sugar, or raisins. Then bake it for 12 to 14 minutes.

·ROLLED-OAT RIDDLE COOKIES·

Bake some **Q** (for **QUESTION**) and **A** (for **ANSWER**) cookies.

Then pass your friends a **Q** cookie and ask them a riddle. If they know the

answer, they get the **A** cookie. If they don't, you get to enjoy it!

WHAT YOU NEED:

1/2 cup (125 mL or 1 stick) butter or
   margarine, softened

3/4 cup (175 mL) white sugar

1 egg

1 teaspoon (5 mL) vanilla extract

1 tablespoon (15 mL) milk

11/2 cups (375 mL) all-purpose flour

1/4 teaspoon (1 mL) baking soda

1/2 cup (125 mL) rolled oats

1/4 teaspoon (1 mL) salt

1/4 cup (50 mL) semisweet miniature
   chocolate chips

cooking spray or extra butter for
   greasing the cookie sheet

WHAT YOU DO:

1 Mix the butter and sugar together in a big bowl until they are creamy.

2 Add the egg, vanilla extract, and milk to the bowl. Mix again.

3 In another bowl, stir the flour, baking soda, rolled oats, and salt together.

4 Bit by bit, add the flour-and-oat mixture to the bowl with the butter mixture and mix until smooth.

5 Stir in the chocolate chips.

6 Pat the dough into a ball and wrap it in plastic wrap or waxed paper. Put the dough in the freezer for about 15 minutes.

7 Preheat the oven to 350°F (180°C). Grease your cookie sheet with the cooking spray or extra butter.

• F O R   M O R E   F U N •

Put craft sticks in your riddle cookies before you bake them so you will have some handles to hold on to.

8 Roll out the dough on a floured surface until it is half as thick as your Alphabake cookie

cutters. Cut out the dough, using the **Q** and **A** Alphabake letters.

9 Gently remove the extra dough around the dough letters. Put the cookies on your cookie sheet, leaving a space as wide as three of your fingers between each one.

10 Bake the cookies for about 10 to 12 minutes. Let the cookies cool before eating.

·RIDDLES TO MAKE YOU AND YOUR FRIENDS GIGGLE·

Q: What's the noisiest way to eat soup?

A: With quackers.

Q: What's brown, hairy, and wears sunglasses?

A: A coconut on vacation.

Q: What do you get when
a dinosaur walks through your vegetable garden?

A: Squash.

Q: What starts with **T**,
ends with **T**, and is full of **T**?

A: A teapot.

·SILLY SNAKE SPICE COOKIES·

S is the letter that the word **SNAKE** starts with.

It's also the sound a snake makes and the shape of a snake!

These snakes won't bite you–but you can bite them!

WHAT YOU NEED:

1/2 cup (125 mL or 1 stick) butter or
  margarine, softened
3/4 cup (175 mL) white sugar
1 egg
1 teaspoon (5 mL) vanilla extract
1 1/2 cups (375 mL) all-purpose flour
1/2 teaspoon (2 mL) baking powder
1 teaspoon (5mL) cinnamon
1/2 teaspoon (2 mL) nutmeg
1/2 teaspoon (2 mL) cloves
1/4 teaspoon (1 mL) salt
cooking spray or extra butter for
  greasing the cookie sheet

WHAT YOU DO:

1 Mix the butter and sugar together in a big bowl until they are creamy.

2 Add the egg and vanilla extract to the bowl. Mix again.

3 In another bowl, stir the flour, baking powder, cinnamon, nutmeg, cloves, and salt together.

4 Bit by bit, add the flour mixture to the bowl with the butter mixture and mix until smooth.

5 Pat the dough into a ball and wrap it in plastic wrap or waxed paper. Put the dough in the freezer for about 15 minutes.

6 Preheat the oven to 350°F (180°C). Grease your cookie sheet with the cooking spray or extra butter.

7 Roll out the dough on a floured surface until it is half as thick as your Alphabake cookie cutters. Cut out the dough, using the letter **S**.

8 Gently remove the extra dough around the dough letters. Put the cookies on your cookie sheet, leaving a space as wide as three of your fingers between each one.

9 Bake the cookies for about 10 to 12 minutes. Let the cookies cool before eating.

· **Try This** ·

Can you say this tongue twister six times quickly?

SIX SHY SNAKES SHAKE SOFT SHINY SHOES

·COCOA COOKIE KISSES·

The letters **X** and **O** are often used by people
when they write to each other as a way to send kisses and hugs.
You can send kisses and hugs to people you like by
making them cookies in these shapes!

WHAT YOU NEED:

1/2 cup (125 mL or 1 stick) butter or
    margarine, softened
3/4 cup (175 mL) white sugar
1 egg
1 teaspoon (5 mL) vanilla extract
11/2 cups (375 mL) all-purpose flour
1/2 teaspoon (2 mL) baking powder
1/4 cup (50 mL) unsweetened cocoa
1/4 teaspoon (1 mL) salt
cooking spray or extra butter for
    greasing the cookie sheet

WHAT YOU DO:

1 Mix the butter and sugar together in
a big bowl until they are creamy.

2 Add the egg and vanilla extract to
the bowl. Mix again.

3 In another
bowl, stir the
flour, baking
powder, cocoa,
and salt together.

4 Bit by bit, add the flour mixture to the bowl with the butter mixture and mix until smooth.

5 Pat the dough into a ball and wrap it in plastic wrap or waxed paper. Put the dough in the freezer for about 15 minutes.

6 Preheat the oven to 350°F (180°C). Grease your cookie sheet with the cooking spray or extra butter.

7 Roll out the dough on a floured surface until it is half as thick as your Alphabake cookie cutters. Cut out the dough, using the letters **X** and **O**.

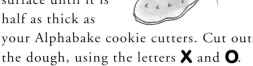

8 Gently remove the extra dough around the dough letters. Put the cookies on your cookie sheet, leaving a space as wide as three of your fingers between each one.

9 Bake the cookies for about 10 to 12 minutes. Let the cookies cool before eating.

● ● ● ● ● ● ●

•FOR MORE FUN•

You can make your kisses and hugs extra chocolaty by putting chocolate sprinkles on them before baking!

·PLAY TIC-TAC-TOE·

You can also use the letters **X** and **O**
to play a game of tic-tac-toe. You'll need some paper,
a crayon or pencil, and a friend to play with.

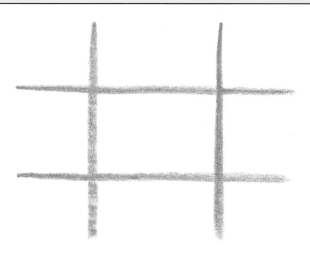

·What You Do·

....

1 Copy the game board shown here on a piece of paper.

2 Decide who will draw the **X**s,
who will draw the **O**s, and who will go first.

3 Take turns writing the letter you have picked in one of the spaces.
If you draw a big game board, you can put your Alphabake **X** or **O** cookie
cutter right on the paper and trace around it when it's your turn.

4 The first person to fill three spaces in a row with
his or her letter going across, down, or diagonally is the winner!

·BOO COOKIES·

These cookies make up a word you'll hear
on Halloween, and they have a surprise in them, too. When you
give them to your friends, you can say **BOO**!

WHAT YOU NEED:

$1/2$ cup (125 mL or 1 stick) butter or
margarine, softened

$3/4$ cup (175 mL) white sugar

1 egg

1 teaspoon (5 mL) vanilla extract

2 teaspoons (10mL) grated orange rind

$1^1/2$ cups (375 mL) all-purpose flour

$1/2$ teaspoon (2 mL) baking powder

$1/4$ teaspoon (1 mL) salt

$1/4$ cup (50 mL) hard orange candies

tinfoil

WHAT YOU DO:

1 Mix the butter and sugar together in a big bowl until they are creamy.

2 Add the egg, vanilla extract, and orange rind to the bowl. Mix again.

3 In another bowl, stir the flour, baking powder, and salt together.

4 Bit by bit, add the flour mixture to the bowl with the butter mixture and mix until smooth.

5 Pat the dough into a ball and wrap it in plastic wrap or waxed paper. Put the dough in the freezer for about 15 minutes.

6 Preheat the oven to 350°F (180°C). Cover your cookie sheet with tinfoil.

7 Ask a grown-up to break the orange candies into small pieces. Set the broken-up candies aside.

8 Roll out the dough on a floured surface until it is half as thick as your Alphabake cookie cutters. Cut out the dough, using the letters **B** and **O**. Be sure to cut out twice as many **O**s as **B**s.

9 Gently remove the extra dough around the dough letters. Put the cookies on your foil-covered cookie sheet, leaving a space as wide as three of your fingers between each one.

10 Fill in the holes in your cookie letters with the broken candies.

11 Bake the cookies for about 10 to 12 minutes, checking them to make sure the candy doesn't burn.

12 Cool the cookies on the sheet for 15 minutes, then peel them off the foil.

WARNING: Do **NOT** touch the melted candy when it is hot or you will burn yourself.

• F O R   M O R E   F U N •

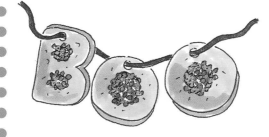

Before you bake your **BOO** cookies, use a straw to poke a hole through the top of each letter. After the cookies have cooled, run some ribbon or string through the holes you have made and hang up your **BOO** cookies as decorations.

·DOUBLE DELICIOUS COOKIES·

These cookies are twice as good as any
other cookie. Why? Each one is made of two cookies held
together with a lemon filling!

WHAT YOU NEED:

**any cookie recipe from the first
half of this book**
1 3/4 cups (425 mL) icing sugar
1/4 cup (50mL) butter, softened
1 tablespoon (15 mL) water
1 tablespoon (15 mL) lemon juice

WHAT YOU DO:

1 Make the cookies by following the recipe. You can use any Alphabake letters you like when you are cutting out the dough — just make sure you bake two of each letter.

2 When the cookies are cool, match up each pair of cookie letters and put them back on the cookie sheet.

3 To make the cookie filling, first mix together the sugar and butter.

4 Beat in the water and lemon juice.

5 Glue each pair of cookies together with the filling so the cookies match.

·ALPHABET EYE SPY·

Can you find 6 things here that start with the letter **D**?
(Answers can be found on page 2.)

25

·ALPHABAKE BISCUITS·

You can make biscuits with your Alphabake letters, too!
They taste great with peanut butter, jam, or cheese. You can also float
them in soup to make your own alphabet soup!

WHAT YOU NEED:

2 cups (500 mL) all-purpose flour
1 tablespoon (15 mL) baking powder
1/2 teaspoon (2 mL) salt
1/4 cup (50 mL or 1/2 stick) butter,
   softened
3/4 cup (175 mL) milk

WHAT YOU DO:

1 Preheat the oven to 450°F (230°C).

2 Stir the flour, baking powder, and salt together in a bowl.

3 Add the butter. Rub the butter-and-flour mixture between your fingers until it looks like bread crumbs.

4 Bit by bit, stir in the milk with a fork until the dough sticks together in a ball. (You may not have to use all the milk.)

5 Roll out the dough on a floured surface until it is half as thick as your Alphabake cookie cutters. Cut out the dough, using any of your Alphabake letters.

6 Gently remove the extra dough around the dough letters. Put the biscuits on your cookie sheet, leaving a space as wide as three of your fingers between each one.

7 Bake the biscuits for about 12 minutes. Let the biscuits cool before eating.

·Try These Tasty Treats·

You can eat your biscuits with all these foods.

Can you tell what letter each of these foods begins with?

(Answers can be found on page 2.)

_ OUP

_ AM

_ EANUT BUTTER

_ ILK

Can you make biscuits in these letter shapes?

·PLAY-B-C DOUGH·

This dough is for playing, not eating. You can mold it
with your hands to make letters in the same shapes as your Alphabake
letters. Or you can roll the dough out flat (like a piece of paper)
and print letters and words on it. Just press your Alphabake letters on the
dough, then lift them up. What letter shapes do you leave behind?

WHAT YOU NEED:

3/4 cup (175 mL) all-purpose flour
1/3 cup (75 mL) salt
2 tablespoons (25 mL) cream of tartar

2/3 cup (150 mL) water
2 tablespoons (25 mL) vegetable oil
a variety of food coloring

WHAT YOU DO:

1 Pick the food coloring you want
to add to your dough and set it aside.

2 In a medium-
sized pot, stir
the flour, salt,
and cream of tartar
together.

3 In a bowl, mix the water, oil,
and food coloring together.

4 Pour the bowl
into the pot and stir
everything together
until there are no lumps.

5 Stir over medium heat
for about 5 minutes. Scrape the
bottom and sides of
the pot as you stir.

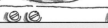

6 When the dough sticks together in a ball, take it off the stove and let it cool for 5 to 10 minutes before you touch it.

7 Squish, squeeze, and squash your dough with your hands. Now it's ready to use with your Alphabake letters.

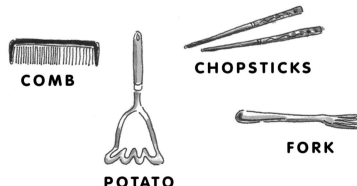

· **Handy Hint** ·
....

When you're finished playing

with your dough, put it in a plastic

bag or container with a lid and

keep it in the refrigerator so that it

doesn't dry out.

· FOR MORE FUN ·

Use these things to make patterns in your play dough!

COMB

CHOPSTICKS

POTATO MASHER

FORK

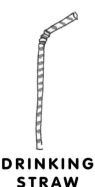

DRINKING STRAW

·HEY DIDDLE DIDDLE DOUGH·

**The barnyard animals that you make
from this play dough can be baked, but not eaten.**

WHAT YOU NEED:

**4 cups (1000 mL) all-purpose flour
1 cup (250 mL) salt
1¹/2 cups (375 mL) warm water**

WHAT YOU DO:

1 Pick out the letters that form the words for the animals in the nursery rhyme (see above). Set the letters aside.

2 Preheat the oven to 300°F (150°C).

3 Mix the flour and salt together.

4 Add the water and mix well with your hands.

·A Nursery Rhyme·

Hey diddle diddle,

The **CAT** and the fiddle,

The **COW** jumped over the moon.

The little **DOG** laughed

To see such sport,

And the dish ran away with the spoon!

5 Roll out the dough until it is half as thick as your Alphabake cookie cutters. Cut out the dough, using the letters you have picked.

6 Gently remove the extra dough around the dough letters. Put the dough letters on your cookie sheet.

7 Stick the edges of the letters in each word together by dabbing them with water and pressing them together.

8 Decorate each word so that it looks like the animal it stands for. Can you add dough whiskers to the word **CAT**?

9 Bake in the oven for about one hour.

·Try This·
....
Can you tell what each animal is saying? Think about the sounds these animals usually make, then say the sounds out loud. Can you make these words out of dough, using your Alphabake letters?

·FOR MORE FUN·

Squeeze some dough through a garlic press to make hair or fur for your animals. You can also glue on wiggly eyes after you bake them.

·MORE THINGS YOU CAN DO WITH YOUR ALPHABAKE LETTERS·

Play with them in the bathtub. The letters will float!

Take the letters and cookie sheet in the car with you. Look at the letters on the license plates of the cars around you. Now find the same letters on your sheet!

Make delicious gelatin letters. Ask a grown-up to make some extra-firm fruit-flavored gelatin. After it has chilled, use your Alphabake letters to cut out gelatin shapes.

Practice your printing. Put your letters on a sheet of paper, then trace around them with a pencil or a crayon.

● ● ● ● ● ● ● ● ● ● ● ● ●

Be sure to wash your letters when you're ready to bake cookies again!